Pignic

Anne Miranda

Illustrations by Rosekrans Hoffma

D1416704

BOYDS MILLS PRESS

To Saturnino
with salsa!—A.M.

For Eileen —R.H.

Text copyright © 1996 by Anne Miranda
Illustrations copyright ©1996 by Rosekrans Hoffman
Alphabet Font copyright © 1996 by Zaner-Bloser, Inc.

Published by Boyds Mills Press, Inc.
A Highlights Company
815 Church Street
Honesdale, Pennsylvania 18431
Printed in China

Publisher Cataloging-in-Publication Data
Miranda, Anne.
    Pignic ; an alphabet book in rhyme / by Anne Miranda ; illustrated by Rosekrans Hoffman.—1st ed.
[32]p. : col. ill. ; cm.
Summary: Pigs gather for their annual picnic in this rhyming alphabet book.
ISBN 1-59078-328-X
1. Children's poetry, American. 2. Alphabet rhymes—Juvenile poetry.
3. Alphabet—Juvenile poetry. [1. American poetry. 2. Alphabet rhymes—poetry. 3. Alphabet.]
I. Hoffman, Rosekrans, ill. II. Title.
808.81—dc20   1996   AC
Library of Congress Catalog Card Number 95-78287

First Boyds Mills Press paperback edition, 2005
Book designed by Kirchoff/Wohlberg, Inc.
The text of this book is set in 30-point Goudy.
The illustrations are done in pencil and colored inks.

10 9 8 7 6 5 4 3 2 1

The annual family pignic
came only once a year.

With picnic baskets on their arms,
pigs came from far and near.

Auntie Anne made apple pie.

Bb

Ben brought beans from Boston.

Cc

Cousin Cabe baked carrot cake.

Some dates arrived with Dustin.

Ee

Evan cooked eel and eggplant stew.

Fern fried fifty fish.

Gg

Gram made cold gazpacho soup.

Hank had a hominy dish.

Ii

Ivan churned the ice cream.

June brought jam in jars.

Karl made pickled kumquat mousse,

and the lemon tarts were Lars'.

Mm

May made mush and meatballs.

Niles brought nectarines.

Ollie stirred the onion sauce.

18

Pp

Paul picked peas and greens.

Qq

Grampa Quigly sliced some quince.

Ray steamed pots of rice.

Ss

Sister Seti strained spaghetti.

Tyler's tea was iced.

Uu

Una brought some ugly fruit.

Violet brought vermicelli.

Walt carved watermelon boats.

Max took extra jelly.

Yolanda mashed some yellow yams.

Zak baked zucchini bread.

"It's the finest pignic ever!"

That's what everybody said.

A a	 apple pie		N n	nectarines
B b	beans		O o	onion sauce
C c	carrot cake		P p	peas
D d	dates		Q q	quince
E e	eggplant stew		R r	rice
F f	fish		S s	spaghetti
G g	gazpacho soup		T t	tea
H h	hominy dish		U u	ugly fruit
I i	ice cream		V v	vermicelli
J j	jam		W w	watermelon
K k	kumquat mousse		X x	extra jelly
L l	lemon tarts		Y y	yams
M m	meatballs		Z z	zucchini bread